Under the Netherfield Mistletoe

A Pride & Prejudice Variation Novella

Abigail Reynolds

WHITE SOUP PRESS

Contents

Chapter 1

ELIZABETH PROWLED THROUGH THE orchard. Where was it, the apple tree the Netherfield gardener had pointed out to her? She had noted it then, but the trees had been just beginning to lose their leaves, a few late fruits still dangling from the twigs. Now they were nothing but bare branches, and everything looked different.

If anything, it should make her quarry stand out more. She huffed out a breath that steamed in the cold air. It must be here somewhere. This morning she had learned the hard way that her judgment was faulty and her vanity overwhelming, but surely she ought to be able to find a single tree!

A glint of green high in the branches caught her eye. Yes, there it was! A cluster of leaves and white berries nestled in the fork where a limb met the trunk. For the first time since she had heard the devastating, mortifying news, a smile crept over her face. Everyone might be laughing at her behind their hands, but at least Longbourn would have the prized greenery to decorate the house this year.

Sometimes the small successes were what mattered.

She waded through the long grass to the base of the tree and glanced around. No one was in sight, thank heavens. She could scramble up the tree to collect her prize – except the first gnarled branch was out of her reach. Curse her luck! She pounded her fist against the rough, grayish bark.

But wait – had she not seen a ladder by the gate? She hurried back to the stone wall. Yes, there it was, an old one no doubt left by whoever had harvested the apples. The top had broken off it, leaving only five rungs and a jagged end, but it would be enough to get her into the branches.

Moss stained the sides, so she stripped off her fine kid gloves before trying to lift it. No point in making her day any worse by ruining her favorite gloves! It was heavier than she expected, but somehow she managed to drag it to the tree. Breathing heavily, she propped it against the trunk.

Where it promptly toppled over.

Oh, bother! She heaved it up again, but even before she let go, the ladder began to list again. She leaned down to examine the base of it. No wonder – one leg had broken off right at the bottom. A good two inches were missing. That would explain why it had been left behind.

It was never going to stand up by itself. She could try to make a hole for the longer leg to go in, but she had nothing to dig with. Or she could put a rock under the short leg... No, then it would fall over when she was atop it, and she would be in far worse straits.

Just then a figure appeared on the path beside the orchard, a woman wrapped in a hooded cloak with her hands stuffed in a fur muff. Not someone she recognized, but she need not be an acquaintance to ask her to hold a ladder for five minutes! That was the answer.

She let the ladder fall again. "Miss?" she called.

The figure turned like a startled rabbit. "Oh! I did not see you!" It was a girl several years younger than her.

Elizabeth forged ahead, despite the embarrassment of soliciting a mere stranger for assistance. "Forgive me, but might I beg a favor of you? I am in desperate need of someone to steady a ladder for me while I pluck a bit of mistletoe from that tree." She pointed behind her.

The girl's eyes widened. "I am so sorry. I am not supposed to speak to anyone!" She sounded terrified.

"I promise not to tell a soul I saw anyone here, and I would be ever so much in your debt," Elizabeth pleaded. "It will only take a minute."

"I should not...."

"Truly, I will say nothing. I would not even press you except that I have been having the most horrible day, and getting this mistletoe will make it a little bit better."

The stranger bit her lip. "I suppose it would not hurt." She made it sound like a question. "And I am sorry you have had a hard day."

"Thank you so much! It is right over here."

The girl followed her and listened carefully to Elizabeth's explanation of the problem. Together they found a place where the short end of the ladder would rest on one of the tree roots protruding from the ground, making it closer to level. Then, with the stranger holding it in place. Elizabeth climbed up it until she could reach the first branch.

It had been some years since she had climbed a tree, but her old skills came back quickly. Soon she reached the branch which held the mistletoe. She pulled out her gardening shears and cut off a cluster, careful to leave enough to grow back. After wrapping the stem in her handkerchief to keep the sticky resin from her skin, she started to clamber back down.

Why was going down always scarier than going up? She had forgotten that little detail of tree climbing, how the view of the ground so far below made her head spin. Still, it was a challenge she relished, even if by the time she felt around for the top step of the ladder with her foot, her heart was pounding. But she had made it!

One step, then two. The ladder gave an ominous crack when Elizabeth reached the third rung. Before it could break completely, she jumped off. Naturally, since she was in front of a well-bred stranger, she tumbled to the ground, landing in a position that guaranteed she would be uncomfortable sitting down for Christmas dinner. She burst out laughing at her predicament.

"Oh, no! Are you hurt?" The girl's eyes were wide.

"Only my dignity! But look, I got it!" She held up her prize triumphantly. "The magical mistletoe of Netherfield, and it is ours!"

"Magical? Why? Is mistletoe so hard to find here?" the girl asked.

"Harder than some places, though boys who climb the old oaks can often find some. But the mistletoe of Netherfield's orchard has long been reputed to bring the best luck. Before they left, the Townsends always held a Christmas ball which often resulted in an unusual number of courtships and marriages. Everyone joked that the amazing Netherfield mistletoe was to blame for it. But then the Townsends left and put the place up for let, and that Christmas some boys came and took every last trace of mistletoe here and sold it as the magical Netherfield mistletoe, so there has been none since then."

"But..." her voice trailed off, faced with the obvious evidence.

Elizabeth laughed. "No one knows about this. When I was visiting Netherfield last month, a gardener pointed this hidden clump out to me. Since the new tenants have left Netherfield, I decided no one would miss a small sprig of it. Even if it is not magical, it would bring a little hope to my family, which badly needs it."

"I am sorry to hear it," the girl said.

"Oh, it is nothing terrible! But my eldest sister has just been abandoned by the suitor we thought would marry her, and I was... well, not exactly being courted by a man, but the entire town knew I was his favorite, and I discovered only today that he was horribly deceitful. Not only to me, but to everyone, even though he seemed the most charming man in the world. That is why I am so out of sorts today and ready to climb a tree." She had not meant to say all of that, especially not to a complete stranger, nor had she intended for her voice to shake when she spoke of that devil George Wickham.

"Oh!" the girl gasped, her eyes suddenly shiny. "I am so, so sorry. There is nothing so horrible as when you trust a man who says he loves you and then find out he is lying."

Elizabeth pulled herself from her own distress long enough to notice that she had not in fact said that Wickham had loved her. Clearly this poor child was thinking of an experience of her own. What wicked man had broken her heart? Was that why she was so pale and wan?

At least Wickham had not fully invaded her own heart. No, her blow was much more to her pride. Vindictively she kicked at the base of the apple tree. "This to lying men! I hope he rots in his own midden."

The stranger looked at her with wide eyes. "In a dunghill," she said in a whisper, as if it were the first time in her life she had ever dared voice such a thought. "I hope someone breaks his heart and takes everything he holds dear, so he can learn what it feels like."

"Yes!" Elizabeth exclaimed. "I have been trying to think of the perfect thing to say to him if he should ever cross my path again." Not that it was likely, after he had been caught with Colonel Foster's new bride, damn him. He would never dare show his face in Meryton now. "Perhaps 'It is a shame that a handsome face and charming manner should be wasted on a man with no morals or honor.' But that is not quite insulting enough, is it?"

"No, he deserves worse, that horrid man! But what more can we do? What remedy does a woman have for a cad who has broken her faith? How can we ever believe someone who says they love us again?" Despair poured out in her words.

"I admit I will not give my trust to a man as freely in the future," Elizabeth said slowly. "But I refuse to let him triumph over me or take away my ability to love." She held up the sprig in her hand. "And that is where this comes in."

Her brow wrinkled. "By trying to catch the interest of another man? But what if he is just as much of a deceiver?"

"No. By refusing to give up hope, even if I cannot imagine another man right now. Mr.... The cad would think himself a very fine fellow if he knew he had the power to make me give up on men, or even to make me hopeless and miserable. I will not give him that."

"But how? I am hurt. How can I deny it?"

The poor girl! "You cannot deny your feelings. They are real and true. But you *can* decide not to let a bounder ruin your life. You can remember that there is hope, even if you cannot feel it right now." Elizabeth dropped the mistletoe into her basket. "Do you know why we bring greenery into our houses at Christmastime? The tradition is far older than Christianity. It is to remind us that even in the darkest, coldest time of the year, there is still green. Spring will come someday, no matter how impossible that might seem when the plants are brown and dead. Even if it feels like your heart will never heal." She took a deep breath. "Do not let any man take that away from you. There is a bit of greenery even in the deepest winter."

The girl wrung her hands. "I came here to escape from Christmas. Everyone in Town kept talking about gaiety and parties, all the joy of the season. And there is no joy in my heart."

How well she understood that! "I ran from my family today because I could not keep a smile on my face any longer. No doubt at Christmas I shall force myself to do so and pretend to a gaiety I do not possess, but I will also look at the evergreen boughs hung over the mantel and remind myself that spring will come. And I will think of even more horrible things to say to that selfish man who cares for nothing but himself. I will say in my mind, 'Good riddance to you! I do not care this much for a miserable excuse for a human being like you!'" She snapped her fingers.

"Yes, good riddance!" The smallest of smiles broke through her somber expression. "Good riddance!" Clearly she was relishing the words.

It felt good to encourage this shy child, so she said, "And while I am looking at that green bough, I will say 'good riddance' to your horrid man, too, and think of throwing him in a pig midden!"

The stranger said, "I will do the same for yours! Though we have no greenery, since I wanted no reminders of Christmas." She sounded wistful.

Elizabeth tilted her head to the side. "If I cut you one small green bough, will you put in on your mantelpiece so we can share that moment?"

A reckless glint came into her eyes. "I will put up all the evergreens! For you are right, that they have a different meaning." She hesitated. "And I think my brother would like it, too."

Elizabeth held up her garden shears. "Then let us cut greenery and wish our evil men into a cesspool!"

Chapter 2

D ARCY HANDED OFF HIS horse to the groom he had brought with him from London. Using Netherfield servants would increase the likelihood someone in the neighborhood would discover his presence there, and that would not do. The last thing he wanted was callers, not when he was trying to provide Georgiana with a complete retreat from society.

It would have been better to go somewhere they were both unknown, but it had been hard to find a house elsewhere on short notice at Christmas. Georgiana had wanted desperately to get away from everyone. When Bingley had offered him the secluded cottage at Netherfield, it seemed heaven-sent.

Even if it had meant disposing of Wickham's presence in Meryton, just to be on the safe side, but that blackguard's proximity to the bewitching Miss Elizabeth Bennet had been nagging at him since he had first left Netherfield. Even if Darcy could never have her, he did not want her to fall victim to Wickham's schemes. Fortunately it had only been a matter of sending a solicitor to speak to Wickham's colonel with evidence of his past behavior. It had been a bonus when Colonel Forster sent for Wickham to answer the charges, and Wickham was found in flagrante with the new Mrs. Forster.

Darcy strode towards the cottage. How had Georgiana managed without him, all alone except for the maid and the cook? He had hated to leave her in such low spirits, even for half a day.

But as he opened the door, a sound came to meet him, one he had not heard in months, not since the disaster at Ramsgate and Georgiana's rapid decline afterwards. It was the sound of his sister laughing. Giggling, to be precise.

It could not be. When he had left this morning, she had been on the verge of tears, as usual. What miracle was this?

Then, as he stepped towards the drawing room, an all-too-familiar musical voice wafted past him. An unforgettable voice, one which haunted his dreams. But what was *she* be doing here?

She could ruin everything - even though he ached to see her.

"Will this be close enough to the hearth that you can throw the ash pail at any nasty, lying man?" Her tone was full of laughter, just as he remembered it.

"It is perfect," Georgiana replied. "Though I still would prefer it to be pig dung."

Pig dung? His delicate, depressed little sister was talking about *pig dung* to an absolute stranger?

Elizabeth's tinkling laugh sent a rush of desire through him.

"Oh, yes, that would be better - if we do not count having to tolerate the smell of it the rest of the time. What about pouring the ashes over him, and while he is blinded by that, finding a nice, full chamber pot to empty over his head? Would that not be fitting?"

The response was another fit of giggles.

Darcy closed his mouth, which had fallen open at this remarkably odd conversation. And he could no longer help himself. He had to see her.

He sidled over to the open drawing room door. There she was, standing on tiptoe on a tall stool, her well-turned ankles exposed as she raised her arms high to tie something to the blackened ceiling beam. The sunlight through the window behind her outlined her shape in loving detail through the blue muslin dress.

Darcy swallowed hard. It was all he could do not to rush over, pull her into his arms, and make his secret dreams reality.

He had no business thinking of Elizabeth Bennet like this. Yet here she stood, as if they were a family decorating for Christmas, laughing with his sister. How he wished it could be true!

"There!" she cried triumphantly. "What do you think?"

He could not take his eyes off her. The woman who had so bewitched him, whom he had forced himself to leave, whom he had never thought to see again. Standing in the sunlight in all her glory, her face alight as she smiled at his sister.

He must have made some sort of noise, for Georgiana started and looked over at him. "Oh! Brother, I did not expect you so soon. Do not fear, I did not tell her my name, and she has promised to keep my presence here a secret."

Elizabeth, still on tiptoe, turned her head abruptly towards him. Her luscious lips made a little circle of surprise - and then she lost her balance. Her arms flailed to the side, and she began to topple.

He rushed forward and caught her, lowering her until her feet rested securely on the ground. None too quickly; this remarkable taste of pleasure in holding Elizabeth Bennet in his arms would have to last him a lifetime. The warmth of her soft body sent a surge of delight through him.

Reluctantly - oh, so reluctantly - he released his grip on her. "Are you hurt?" he asked, striving to keep his voice modulated, as if this miracle was an everyday occurrence that had no effect on him.

She gave a breathy laugh, her color becomingly high. "My dignity is severely sprained, but I am otherwise unharmed." With a droll expression, added, "How mortifying! That of all the young ladies I might encourage to imagine throwing ill-behaved men into the pig slops, I chose your genteel and well-bred sister. I am clearly a bad influence, and should take my leave instantly in order to limit the damage."

"Oh, no!" Georgiana cried. "I have so enjoyed our conversation. Truly, Brother, she has been everything that is kind to me – and delightful company, too."

"I thank you for your spirited defense! Unfortunately for me, your brother is already well aware of my many sins, and knows a great deal to my disadvantage," Elizabeth said with mock ruefulness. "He already thinks me ill-bred and prone to improper behavior."

Darcy could not help but smile. How he had missed crossing verbal swords with her! "Fear not, Georgiana. Miss Elizabeth Bennet finds great enjoyment in occasionally professing opinions which in fact are not her own."

Georgiana's eyes grew wide. "Oh, no! You know each other? And *this* is Miss Elizabeth Bennet, who you mentioned in your letters to me?"

Elizabeth dropped a curtsey. "Guilty as charged, m'lord. But you may keep calling me Helena if you wish."

"Helena?" he asked, baffled.

She tilted her head with a teasing look. "Your sister quite properly would not reveal her name to me, but it would have been terribly rude to call her 'whoever you may be.' Since we were traipsing through the woods like the young ladies in A Midsummer Night's Dream, we decided she would be Hermia and I Helena. I think your sister makes quite a delightful Shakespearean heroine, do you not agree?"

Darcy would have agreed to change his own name if it made her lovely eyes sparkle like that. "I hope I will not have to play the part of Bottom the Weaver, with the head of a donkey."

She waved her hand. "No, we are saving our venom today for blackguards and cads, so you are perfectly safe from us. But I believe I have quite overstayed my welcome here, so I will take my leave. I have already promised your sister that I will tell no one of her presence here, and I will happily extend that to you as well." She dropped her voice conspiratorially. "After all, any mention of it would reflect much worse on me! Especially as our acquaintance started with your sister discovering me in the act of larceny."

"For shame, Miss Elizabeth," he said in an air of mock disapproval. "What did you steal?"

She gestured to the basket on the side table. "Sprigs of the magical Netherfield mistletoe. And a few branches of greenery, which are now on your mantel, making you an accessory to my crime."

"A terrible crime indeed, but I may be able to persuade Bingley not to prosecute you. Just this one time." He could not resist prolonging the conversation - anything to prevent a final goodbye. Even this brief reprieve of basking in her presence for a few minutes had brought a part of him back to life, blossoming in the mid-winter.

Georgiana said timidly, "You are not angry that I spoke to her? Or that we put up greenery, even after I said I wanted nothing to remind me of Christmas? Helena - I mean, Miss Bennet says that the greens are a reminder that spring will come again, no matter how dark and cold it is now." She hesitated. "It was not all about dunking gentlemen in pig dung."

"On the contrary, I am delighted you found Miss Elizabeth. I will go so far as to agree with her, that there are some men who would benefit greatly from having a much closer acquaintance with pig dung."

Elizabeth gave him a sly look. "Though I daresay you might avoid saying so in public, and to a complete stranger."

"Perhaps so," he acknowledged, "but if I recall my Shakespeare, Helena and Hermia were dear friends of many years standing, not strangers at all."

"There you have it. We were just staying in character, were we not, dearest Hermia?"

Georgiana moved for the first time, coming forward to link her arm with Elizabeth's. "You are right, my old friend Helena." And once again, she laughed. "Pray, Brother, may Miss Bennet stay for refreshments? Mrs. Hudson is making tea."

"I would be honored to have her company." And if Georgiana actually ate a bite of the various delicacies the cook provided to tempt her absent appetite, Darcy might get down on his knees and beg Elizabeth to join them for every single meal. If he could get over his jealousy that his sister had the right to touch Elizabeth when he did not.

"Then I will be glad to remain, if only to further the discussion of the relative merit of pig slops, cow dung, and middens as suitable punishment. I feel I have a great deal to learn on this subject." And her eyes danced again.

"Oh, I simply cannot decide! Which is your favorite, dearest Hermia?" Elizabeth asked Miss Darcy over the tea tray. "Pray, will you not take a taste of these two and let me know which I should choose?" It was not something she would normally say, but given the girl's nearly skeletal appearance, the presence of no less than three cakes on a simple tea tray, and the cook's earlier look of shock and delight when Miss Darcy had requested it, it seemed some encouragement was in order. She had seen people in a decline before.

"Oh, I am certain they are all good," Miss Darcy said hesitantly.

"And you have no appetite, I imagine. Nor do I, to be honest, after my great disappointment. But I refuse to let the cad who deceived me make me ill as well, so I am going to eat this cake to spite him, even if it tastes bad in my mouth. In fact, I think I will take *two* slices, just to show him how little he matters to me." She could not believe she was airing her own disappointment in front of Mr. Darcy, of all people. At least he could not possibly guess that she was speaking of his steward's son, the one who had been so freely maligning him.

Though perhaps she should rethink the accusations Mr. Wickham had made against Mr. Darcy, given all the other lies he had told. The idea made her squirm inside. How could she have been so gullible? Even that awful Caroline Bingley had warned her against Mr. Wickham, and she had deliberately closed her ears to it.

Well, a tiny bit of good might come out of her humiliation if she could use it to strengthen this poor, suffering girl.

Darcy was watching her with a grave expression. "In a spirit of moral support, I will match your two pieces of cake. I would like one of both the almond and the plum cake, Georgiana, if you please."

Georgiana giggled. "That is only because you adore cake."

"Shh. You are giving away my secrets."

Elizabeth tried not to gape. This was a side of Mr. Darcy she had never seen before. Did his sister bring out the best in him?

There might be more to him than she had thought.

Chapter 3

E LIZABETH ROSE TO HER feet. "It will be dark soon, so truly I must go now. My aunt and uncle from London have no doubt already arrived and will be wondering where I am." Hopefully that good reason would forestall Miss Darcy's pleas for her to remain just a little longer. She needed to nurse her pain over Mr. Wickham's perfidy in private, and she was reaching the end of her tolerance for polite company. And then there was the constant stress of wondering what Mr. Darcy was truly thinking of her - and what part he played in convincing Mr. Bingley to leave Netherfield and her dear sister Jane.

"Oh, I hope you will call again!" Miss Darcy exclaimed, with a glance at her brother. "I would be so glad of it."

"Indeed, Miss Elizabeth. I know it must be hard to get away during Christmas, but we would be pleased to see you."

Was he saying that on his own behalf, or simply because she had entertained his sister? It did not matter, after all. The Darcys were only here until Twelfth Night, and then she would never see either of them again. The idea gave her a surprising pang.

"I will do my best. And I promise to keep your presence a complete secret."

Darcy came to stand beside her. "Would you do me the honor of permitting me to accompany you on your walk? As you say, the light is fading."

"It is three miles entire to Longbourn, sir, and it would be full dark long before you are back." And she needed the time alone to recover from this strange day.

He smiled. "I will take a lantern."

"Oh, look!" the girl cried, pointing at the ceiling above their head. "You are under the mistletoe!" She sounded delighted.

Mr. Darcy looked startled, but then a slow smile spread over his countenance. "So we are." No doubt he was making the best of it to please his sister. Elizabeth must be the last woman in the world he would want to find under the mistletoe.

Hastily she said, "I must warn you this is the magic mistletoe of Netherfield. It is unusually potent and should only be used with caution." Not that even Netherfield mistletoe could create a courtship between the proud Mr. Darcy and her!

He raised an eyebrow. "Magical mistletoe?"

She could not resist the opportunity to tease. "Likely it is but an old wives' tale, to be sure. But can you afford to risk it?"

"I think I will take my chances. Unless you object, Miss Elizabeth?" His voice was low.

Her mouth went dry. "I... it is traditional, after all." And she had only herself to blame, since she had hung it there!

"Who am I to break with tradition?" he said in barely a whisper, his eyes growing dark.

Heat rose in her cheeks. She glanced to the side, unable to meet that intent gaze. He would kiss her cheek, would he not?

Then a finger came under her chin, turning her head to face him directly, and his mouth descended on hers.

Her breath caught as an odd feeling churned her insides. Then his lips covered hers, warm, so much softer than she had expected, sending a rush of longing through her. And it was not just a brief brush; his lips clung to hers, as if he were drinking in some essence of her through their caress. It was intimate beyond anything she had ever experienced.

Other young men had occasionally stolen a kiss from her, but it had never felt like this, like something new had come to life deep inside her. She was almost dizzy with it. She wanted to grasp his coat to support herself, to be even closer to him. This vital connection was exquisite, and she longed for more.

Then it was over. The warmth fled from her lips as he raised his head. She opened her eyes to stare at him - when had she closed them? Sometime during that astonishing kiss, which had been eye-opening in every other way.

His breathing was uneven, just like her own. His eyes were soft, even darker now than before. "Yes," he whispered. "That is indeed potent mistletoe."

She rallied her scattered thoughts. "I did warn you."

"So you did." He did not sound displeased, though, far from it.

Could this truly be the same proud, unpleasant Mr. Darcy she had known before, the one who only looked at her to criticize?

Then she came to her senses. What were they doing, staring into each other's eyes after a kiss that had been far more than what was required under the mistletoe - and in front of his young sister? If her cheeks had not already been burning, they certainly would be now!

She rubbed her hands together, trying to force her recalcitrant body to behave. She turned to Miss Darcy, hoping not to see a look of horror on the poor girl's face. Would this have reminded her of kisses from the cad who had betrayed her?

But the girl's hands were clasped together, and her face was alight with hope. Surely she could not believe that kiss had meant something!

Hurriedly Elizabeth said, "And now I truly must depart." Could she sneak off before Mr. Darcy found a lantern? Spending more time in his company right now might be torture of a different sort.

Then she glanced up at him. Would it be such a bad idea? It would give her an opportunity to see if his new agreeability could last through a long, cold walk. After all, she had been completely wrong about Mr. Wickham. Could she have made a similar mistake about Mr. Darcy?

She stole a glance at him. The warmth of his expression kindled hope inside her.

Why had Mr. Darcy insisted on walking with her if he intended not to say a word? It was like the last time she saw him, when they danced together at the Netherfield ball, and she had teased him that they must have some conversation. Apparently that astonishing kiss had not changed anything for him. Or it might had not been as surprising and unusual to him. He must have kissed many women like that, and she was no different from the rest. Or even less than the rest, since his disapproval of her had always been clear.

What if he had only accompanied her in order to remonstrate with her or warn her to stay away from his sister?

With that lowering thought, she gathered her courage. There was one thing she needed to tell him, because it was true. "I do apologize for my interference. I should have left your sister alone when she first said she ought not speak to me."

He gave her a surprised look. "I am glad you did not. Today is the first time I have heard her laugh in nearly half a year. You have my deepest gratitude for that."

What did he want from her, then? "It was a pleasure to meet her. She is a sweet girl."

"Yes." He tightened his greatcoat around him as if the temperature had dropped. "I have a rather odd request to make of you, which may seem impertinent given the conversation we shared during our dance at the Netherfield Ball, but I have only my sister's happiness in mind."

So he remembered that night, too? She had not been under the impression that he had paid the least attention to what she had said then, and she could hardly remember it herself. "I will try not to take offense."

He took a deep breath. "I am aware of your acquaintance with Mr. Wickham. I would greatly appreciate it if you did not mention his name in my sister's presence. She would find it... upsetting."

As if she had any desire to speak of him! The very thought made her stomach lurch, but Mr. Darcy could not know that her opinion had changed so radically. "Of course. I am no longer under the impression that he is a respectable man." Then it struck her. Miss Darcy was devastated by a man who had charmed her, and now this warning from Mr. Darcy. "Oh, no! Was he the one... Oh, I am so sorry! That is none of my business. But what a horrible, horrible thing to do to a vulnerable child."

"My sister has a dowry of thirty thousand pounds." He said it as if that explained everything, which she supposed it did. "It will not be the last time she is targeted by a fortune-hunter, but I wish it had not happened while she was still so young."

Elizabeth had already been angry with Wickham, but now fury filled her. "A dung heap is far too good for him."

"I will not argue the point." He paused, then added, "I think it was rather brilliant of you to make her think he deserves such punishment, though. You seemed to know the right things to say to a young girl." The tone of his voice made an unspoken continuation, that he found the task a hard one.

"Having three younger sisters gives me a great deal of practice," she said. "Though I will admit that your sister listened to me more than mine do!"

"She was lucky to encounter you today," he said seriously.

They had reached a stile, and he offered her his hand to help her cross it. Not that she had failed to do so perfectly well without any assistance only a few hours ago! But she took it, and his touch was like a brand, even through the gloves they both wore. How could she feel such slight pressure through every inch of her body? Truly that kiss had addled her wits!

When Mr. Wickham had taken her hand, she had enjoyed the sensation, but this was so much stronger. How strange, when she did not even like Mr. Darcy!

Or at least she had not before now. Today had showed her a different side of him. Should she give him a second chance?

Except for one thing. As soon as she reached Longbourn, she would see Jane's crestfallen expression, pained by the loss of Mr. Bingley. A loss which Mr. Darcy may well have played a role in.

Should she ask him? It was hardly proper, but nothing she had done that day had been proper. And she cared nothing for his good opinion, did she? At least she had not before today, and he had never hidden his criticism from her. What did she have to lose?

The impulse was too strong for her. "Am I to understand that Mr. Bingley does not plan to return to Netherfield?"

He looked surprised at the change of subject, or it might be at the edge in her voice. "I do not believe so, no."

"A pity. For us, at least, though I doubt it has any effect on him, unlike my poor sister. I had thought better of him, but I suppose there is nothing unusual in a wealthy gentleman leading on a young lady, winning her affection, and then abandoning her. After all, it provides him with entertainment and costs him nothing." Oh, no, that had been too reckless! She had spent too many nights awake wishing she could say that to him, and in her fatigue and disturbance of spirits, the words had tripped too easily off her tongue.

There was silence, and she dared not look at him to judge his expression. Finally he said, "Bingley is a good man, but he falls in and out of love easily and frequently."

"How nice for him! It is unfortunate for the ladies involved, but I suppose their feelings do not matter." She did her best to sound flippant.

"From my observation of the two of them together, your sister's feelings did not seem particularly engaged. Had I thought her in danger, I should have warned Bingley away earlier."

Did he realize what he had just admitted?

Fury rose in her, and she stopped to stare at him. "I am greatly impressed that you can judge so much simply by looking at a woman's face from a distance. Especially when ladies are expected to keep an even countenance at all times! Sadly, this time you were sorely mistaken. A pity Mr. Bingley did not rely on his own judgment in his romantic endeavors; he might have done better."

"If your sister was hurt by his departure, then I am sorry for it."

"If! If! If I was lying in what I said, you mean!" She was beyond rational thought now. "I believe it is time for you to turn back now. That way you can return to your heartbroken sister more quickly while I go to care for mine." That should give him something to think about! She stomped ahead at a quick pace.

He hurried beside her. "Miss Elizabeth, I did not mean to question your word. Especially when you have just been so kind to Georgiana."

Insufferable man! Still, somehow she must rein in her temper. "It is easy to be kind to her. Good day, Mr. Darcy." She put all the finality she could in her words.

This time he did not follow her. "Good day, Miss Elizabeth." He sounded defeated. "I hope we will see you again."

Because he wanted her to cheer his sister, of course. She called back, "I will not break my promise to Miss Darcy."

She set as fast a pace as she dared. Past the fields and around the copse, until she was certain he could not see her. Then she stopped, pressing her hands against her face, trying to still her fast breathing and pounding heart.

What was wrong with her?

Everything, of course. Her own disappointment in Mr. Wickham, learning how fallible her judgment had been. Jane's heartbreak. Even before that, the disaster of Mr. Collins's proposal and her mother's rage that she had refused him. Her shock in discovering that her dear friend Charlotte would betray everything she believed in to marry for money.

One day they had all been happy at the Netherfield ball, where the worst thing that happened was having to dance with that horrid Mr. Darcy. And then, the very next day, everything had gone so wrong so quickly.

Now she had to find a way to restore her countenance before she reached the house. She could not go in there with her temper so unbalanced.

She needed to follow the advice she had given Miss Darcy. It was time to think about the hope of spring.

Chapter 4

HOW HARD COULD IT be? All Elizabeth had to do was to plaster a smile on her face, walk into the cottage at Netherfield, and say all the polite nothings to Miss Darcy and her horrid brother. The one whose kiss had kept her awake at night more than she cared to admit, making her hot all over and longing for more. And to pretend their quarrel had not taken place, or that she had not deliberately provoked it.

Had it been because of that kiss?

She could hear the tinkling sounds of a pianoforte as she approached. Taking a deep breath, she knocked on the door. The maid seemed to be expecting her and showed her into the drawing room.

Her heart gave a little start at the sight of Mr. Darcy, who was sitting at a table writing what appeared to be a letter. He rose immediately and made a stiff bow.

Georgiana jumped up from the pianoforte. "Oh, Miss Bennet! I am so glad you came. Is it not delightful, Brother?"

Her brother looked anything but delighted. "Welcome, Miss Elizabeth. I hope your family is well."

"Very well, I thank you," she said through her suddenly dry mouth. Why should she be surprised that he was not pleased to see her, after the way she had treated him two days ago? And why did it hurt?

He said gravely, "I am happy to hear it. Since you are no doubt here to visit my sister, I pray you excuse me." And without another word, he bowed again and left.

Ouch.

She managed to keep her smile, though. "I cannot stay long, since we have visitors at home, but I wanted to tell you how excited my sisters are to have some of the magical mistletoe of Netherfield. Even though I could not tell them of *our* adventures, dearest Hermia!"

The girl still looked as if she had been ill, but her color was slightly better today. "I have been taking your advice about trying to play music even though I do not feel the desire. It has been helping, I think."

"And it sounds lovely. I wish I could play half so well as what I heard from outside! But one small step at a time."

"Yes," she said. "Even if the steps are hard."

"They are indeed hard! But I brought you something that I want to try." She set her basket on the table and took out a packet of twigs prettily tied up with ribbons. "My aunt, who is visiting from London, has a trick for cleansing pain away at Christmas. You take a scrap of paper and write on it whatever you want to leave behind you. Roll it up and slip it inside the ribbon, and then we cast it into the fire. She helped me make these." She held it out to Miss Darcy.

The girl took it and cradled it in her palms. "I have heard of this before. Some of our neighbors at home do something like this, but we never tried it."

"I should not be surprised. It must be a local custom. My aunt was raised in a town not far from Pemberley."

This seemed to catch her interest. "Truly? Do you have family there, too?"

"I fear not. She is my uncle's wife, and I believe all her family left Lambton after her father died. He was the rector there."

"Lambton? Oh, that is indeed close to Pemberley. It is a small world." Then she seemed to lapse back into her low spirits.

Ever since learning Wickham was responsible for both their woes, Elizabeth had been even more determined to help the girl - no matter how much she might wish to avoid her brother. "Will you join me in this? I truly wish to burn some of my experiences from this year and move forward, and it would mean so much to me if we did it together."

"I will try anything," she said.

"Good. Then let us make our notes. I brought these scraps of paper, and I see your brother has kindly left out ink and a pen for us." Not giving her a chance to object, Elizabeth sat down at the table, carefully choosing the seat Mr. Darcy had not used and pulled off her gloves lest they be stained with ink.

She leaned over to pick up the quill - uncomfortably aware that his fingers had only recently been where hers were now - and dipped it into the ink. She hesitated a moment until she felt Miss Darcy moving behind her, and then she began to write.

"Are you putting down your cad's name?" the girl asked shyly.

"I am just writing 'the blackguard' because I do not want to dirty a perfectly fine piece of paper with his name, or even send ashes with it up the chimney! But not just that; I am also going to include my misplaced pride, which tells me I should be ashamed for failing to see through a man whom everyone else believed, too. Sometimes my own standards of perfection are my worst enemy. I want to learn to forgive myself."

"I know just what you mean," Miss Darcy said with a deep sigh.

Elizabeth held out one of the scraps of paper to her. "Will you do one, too?"

"Yes," Miss Darcy said, with a surprising firmness. "I will burn him to ash, and my self-doubts with it." She sat down in Darcy's seat.

"Good for you!" Elizabeth handed her the pen, careful to keep it away from the half-written letter he had left behind lest she accidentally leave a blot on it. But as she did so, a familiar name jumped out at her from the top of the page.

The letter was to Mr. Bingley.

Suddenly every word of her quarrel with Mr. Darcy rushed back to her, with both anger and embarrassment. Anger at him for what he had done, and mortification that she had lost her temper and behaved in manner that could only confirm his low opinion of her and her family.

And now she was snooping in his letter.

She tore her eyes away from it. There was no reason to read it, anyway. It was just a letter to his friend, nothing to do with her. Instead, she said the first thing that jumped into her mind. "Do you think your brother would like to join us? I brought a third one just in case."

The girl looked up from the blank paper she was frowning over, and her face brightened. "I will ask him."

Elizabeth had asked for him to join them. The words kept echoing in Darcy's head. Had she read the letter he had deliberately left out, the one where he told Bingley he had been wrong about Miss Bennet's sentiments? It had seemed like a sign when she arrived just as he was writing, and on impulse he had left it there where she might notice.

It would be some comfort, during his long, lonely nights, to know she would be thinking a little better of him. That he might make mistakes, but he would repair them.

But this was not the moment to think of how often he dreamed of Elizabeth Bennet. He was supposed to be deciding what he wanted to burn in the fire, and he would never surrender his memories of her, no matter how much she might haunt him.

He picked up the pen. What did he want to leave behind him? Apart from George Wickham, but he had long since realized that particular burr would stick to his coattails forever regardless of what he did. What could he change?

Out of the corner of his eyes, he watched Elizabeth coaxing a smile out of his sister. The one whom none of the finest doctors in London could help, who could not be cheered by any of the well-bred friends he had pressured into visiting her, who could not be pleased by any of the expensive gifts he bought her. Who was finally finding a trace of happiness thanks to Elizabeth Bennet, the woman whom Darcy had judged not good enough for him.

Elizabeth, who had befriended her not in the hope of the favors Darcy could do for her or because she had thought there was an advantage in it, but because she had seen a girl in pain and thought to relieve it. Did he know anyone in fine London society who would have done the same?

He dipped the pen in the ink and wrote quickly, 'Misplaced pride. Judging people based on my first impressions and society's expectations rather than their true worth.' He waved his hand to dry it, then rolled it up tightly and tucked it inside the ribbon. Unlike his letter to Bingley, this was not for Elizabeth's eyes.

What had she written on hers? Surely if his name had been on her list, she would not have invited him to take part in this.

He joined them by the hearth, holding up his packet. "I am ready."

"Excellent," she said. "On the count of three, then. Miss Darcy, will you do the honors?"

How cleverly she had made Georgiana take an active role!

His sister raised her chin. "To new beginnings. One, two, three." She tossed her tied-up twigs into the fire.

Elizabeth followed suit, and his was next, landing almost on top of Elizabeth's. Lucky twigs, to be able to touch hers! If only he had the privilege of being so close to her, even if it meant burning up. He was already on fire for her, after all.

Tendrils of grey smoke rose as the paper was engulfed in flames. Darcy kept his gaze fixed on the ribbons curling and turning black; it was safer than watching Elizabeth. His expression might give too much away.

"Out with the old, in with the new," Elizabeth murmured.

Chapter 5

D ARCY PEERED OUT THE window of the cottage at
the new snow that had fallen overnight. Only an
inch or two, but disappointment fell on him like a weight.
It was Boxing Day, and he had lived in waiting to see her
again. But it would not be today, after all, and might not
even be tomorrow.

Georgiana stepped up beside him. "Will it keep Miss
Bennet from calling today? She said she would."

"Most likely," he acknowledged, the words bitter in his
mouth.

The animation fled from Georgiana's face. "I was looking forward to seeing her," she said, in a ghost of the voice
she had used a moment earlier.

He glanced at her, seeing the telltale signs of her decline. It had been a little better since she met Elizabeth, but it only took a small disappointment to set her back.

What would Elizabeth say if she were here? He tried to imagine it. "I think she is looking out her bedroom window at Longbourn, making plans for when she will be able to see you again. She truly enjoys your company. And then she will see the sun sparkling on the snow, and enjoy the reminder of beauty even in the cold. She might even go out and make a snowball, just for the enjoyment of it."

The idea of Elizabeth playing in snow made him feel better, at least. She would love the deeper snows at Pemberley, where he would wrap her in blankets and take her out in the old sleigh. If only it could be!

Georgiana sighed wistfully. "You are right. She would see the beauty in it."

If only he could see her, with her eyes that sparkled more brightly than the snow in sunshine.

The knock came unexpectedly. As if Darcy had not been hoping against hope for it. As if he had not been close to the point of damning secrecy and marching over to Longbourn to see Elizabeth, snow or no snow. If only he had some way of explaining his presence there!

Let it be her. Let it be her. The refrain repeated in his head as he rose to his feet. Georgiana was faster, though, or less concerned for her dignity. She raced to the door and threw it open. Apparently she did not care about hiding their presence here anymore, either, if it meant seeing Elizabeth one moment sooner.

And there she was, her cheeks flushed and rosy under the hood of the heavy red wool cloak. Snowflakes dotted it, caking at the hem. Another woman would have seemed tired and wan after such a walk, but Elizabeth was deliciously alive and vibrant, as if it had given her energy instead of using it up.

Georgiana cried, "Oh, I am so happy to see you! I did not think you would be able to come today."

"What is a little fresh snow? As your brother can tell you, I once walked to Netherfield after the rain, which was much more troublesome. And I cannot tell you how filthy I was when I arrived – my petticoats were six inches deep in mud!" She gave him an impudent smile, as if daring her to contradict him.

"All I recall is that your eyes were brightened by the exercise," he said. "I hope you took care on your way here. I would not want you to slip and fall."

Now she was definitely laughing at him. "I did, but only once." She turned to display her back, which was indeed covered with snow. "It was rather exciting, as I slid down a small slope. But I am quite unharmed."

Darcy could not take his eyes off her animated features. "I am glad of that. May I take your cloak? I fear the snow has kept our maid away, but I will endeavor to do my best as a substitute."

Elizabeth undid the clasp at her neck. "I thank you."

He stepped behind her, and then carefully reached around her. His heart raced at how close this was to an embrace, and he yearned to make it a true one. Especially after her gloved hand brushed against his fingers as he reached the clasp, sending a surge of desire through him. He lifted the cloak carefully, as if it were the greatest treasure, and only reluctantly relinquished it to the hook by the door. Fortunate garment, to be able to wrap itself around her light and pleasing body, to feel the warmth of her!

Elizabeth favored him with a smile that was greater thanks than any words could be. Especially when he could still feel her touch burning on his hand.

He forced himself to recall where they were and that Georgiana stood only a few feet away. Somehow he managed to say, "Pray come in and sit by the fire to warm yourself. I will ask Cook to make tea." It would give him a much-needed moment to recover his composure. And his sanity. Why was it that he could not make her his wife, to have the right to touch her?

When he returned to the drawing room, Elizabeth was holding out her hands to the fire and saying to Georgiana, "Besides, I could not miss our appointment today, for as it turns out, I am leaving for London tomorrow."

Suddenly he felt as cold as if he had been the one who walked through the snow. So this might be the last time he would see her. Unless Bingley...No, he would not get ahead of himself. He would enjoy this brief time of pleasure in her company. The memory of it might have to last a lifetime.

"Oh." Georgiana's face fell, and she was silent for a moment. "I will be sorry to lose your company."

Elizabeth reached out and took her hand. "It is the only bad part of this unexpected trip, that I will not see you again while you are here. Perhaps someday we can meet again."

This was his moment. He cleared his throat. "That may happen sooner than you think. Bingley is opening up Netherfield again and plans to come here in the New Year. So there may be an opportunity to continue your acquaintance with less secrecy."

Elizabeth turned to stare at him, her eyes wide. "Mr. Bingley is returning?"

"I received a note from him yesterday."

She hesitated, likely counting days in her head. "You wrote to him first," she said, almost as if it were a question.

He inclined his head. "I did." There was no point in denying it, especially if she had peeked at his letter.

"So he had not lost interest in—" She stopped abruptly and glanced at Georgiana, who knew nothing of Bingley and Miss Bennet. "In Netherfield," she finished. A smile bloomed on her face.

"Apparently not," he agreed, drinking in her pleasure at the news.

"That will be good for the neighborhood," she said, clearly speaking of one particular person. "And I shall miss his arrival! But not by much; I will return in late January."

Georgiana was eyeing them with puzzlement. She must have sensed there was more to their conversation than met the eye. He had best change the subject, if he did not want to answer uncomfortable questions later.

"Is there an occasion for your sudden journey, Miss Bennet? I hope it is not unwelcome news."

"Nothing serious. My aunt received word that one of her children is ill, so she and my uncle are going home early. They asked me to join them. Well, actually they asked my sister Jane first, but she has a cold herself and does not want to travel yet, so I will go in her place." She said it almost apologetically. "I almost said no, so as not to miss the festivities here, but in truth it will be a relief to be away. My mother has been in a terrible temper with me this last month, and I am rather tired of it."

"Oh, no!" Georgiana said, looking horrified. "I am sorry she is being unkind to you."

Elizabeth seemed to shake off the serious moment and laughed. "It is my own fault, or so she would say. My poor conduct is a great disappointment to her." But it was clear she found that assessment more amusing than troublesome.

"I cannot believe that," Darcy said, just in case she was more distressed than she was letting them see.

"Oh, it is true!" Now she was definitely teasing. "My terrible behavior is hardly a secret, since she has complained about it to everyone in town, so I might as well tell you what a poor excuse for a daughter I am. I refused a proposal of marriage she wished me to accept, for the sole reason that the man was a fool I could not respect. He will inherit our house after my father dies, though, and that was enough to persuade my mother," she said lightly. "Myself, I have no regrets."

He knew immediately who she meant, and it filled him with fury to think that the man dared raise his eyes to Elizabeth. "My aunt's rector, I assume. You would be wasted on him." The words came out before he realized how improper they were.

She smiled at his discomfort, but kindly, as if understanding him. "From his descriptions of your aunt, I cannot imagine she would be pleased to discover he had married an impertinent miss with no sense of decorum."

"I would hardly describe you that way, Miss Elizabeth," he said. "Still, I do not imagine you would enjoy Lady Catherine's acquaintance greatly."

Her eyes danced. "You would not describe me as impertinent?"

How neatly she had trapped him with the sharp sword of her wit! And how he loved fencing like this with her. "Upon occasion, perhaps" he allowed. "It does not necessarily follow that is always unwelcome."

Georgiana said, "I think you are absolutely wonderful, and I am glad you did not marry that man, for otherwise I would never have met you."

If only Darcy could allow himself to say such things to her! If only he did not have to marry a woman with better connections! But he could not permit himself even to dream of that.

Or that someday he was going to have to face the idea that another man would marry his Elizabeth.

Darcy hated it when Georgiana cried. He was supposed to protect her from anything that would hurt her. He had failed with Wickham, and now again. No matter how brief her acquaintance with Elizabeth was, she was the first person Georgiana had shown any interest in since Ramsgate.

But in this case, he felt as bereft as Georgiana.

"I wish I could at least write to her," his sister sobbed.

"It would be hard to explain, since as far as the rest of the world knows, you have never met her." If people discovered they had been at Netherfield secretly, they would start asking why, and that would draw unwanted attention to Georgiana.

"I know, but I still wish it."

There must be something he could do to help. "Bingley will be living here again soon. When you feel able to be in company again, we could pay him a visit, and then you can be formally introduced to Elizabeth. After that, you can write as much as you want."

And he could see Elizabeth again. A brief taste of happiness, and then even more memories to break his heart over. He would do it, though. It was impossible to resist.

Georgiana dabbed at her eyes with her handkerchief. "Could we?" The relief in her voice made him feel even more guilty, as if somehow he was the one depriving her of her friend.

"When you are ready." Not that there had been any sign of that so far. His sister hated even having the servants see her.

She took a deep breath. "I could start practicing. Maybe paying a call or two, to people whom I know are at least kind."

His sister would never have agreed to such a scheme a week ago, and now she was suggesting it herself. All thanks to Elizabeth and her indomitable spirit. "We can do that," he said, careful not to push her.

She sat silently for a few minutes, and he prayed that she was not going to think better of the plan. Then she said, "I have an idea."

Chapter 6

ELIZABETH HAD ONLY BEEN in London two days when the Gardiner's maid sought her out in the nursery. "You have callers, miss."

Elizabeth looked up from the book she was reading to her little cousin. "For me? Surely they are looking for my aunt." The only people who even knew she was in London were friends of the Gardiners.

"No, they asked for you." The maid held out a card to her. "A gentleman and his sister."

Heat raced through her as she pretended to examine the calling card. No need to read the name, even though her eyes wanted to linger on every letter of it, just like her fingertips wanted to cling to the tiny card that he had touched.

She had been trying so hard to forget him since her arrival in London two days ago, and now he was here. Why? Even at home, where he was well acquainted with her family, he had not called on her, much less bent his pride to appear in Cheapside. And his sister had been avoiding all social contacts. Why was she now seeking out a stranger's household?

And why were they not still at Netherfield? Georgiana had said they were staying through Twelfth Night.

It meant nothing. No doubt Georgiana had wished to see her, and Mr. Darcy had chosen to degrade himself in order to help his sister. He was not the one who was there to see her, and she needed to remember that.

She was not dressed for morning calls. Should she change first? But no, she would not give in to trying to meet impossible expectations; they had seen her when she had been clambering through the Netherfield orchard.

But she would rather not face Mr. Darcy alone. Closing the book and excusing herself, she hurried to Mrs. Gardiner's sitting room and informed her of their illustrious callers.

Mrs. Gardiner's eyebrows shot up. "Mr. Darcy of *Pemberley*? Lizzy, is there something you have not been telling me?"

"No! Nothing like that." Elizabeth pressed her hands to her hot cheeks. "I accidentally befriended his sister, not knowing who she was. She has been through a painful experience recently and has been in something of a decline. When she took a liking to me, he decided to encourage it." Or something like that, if one did not count an astonishing kiss under the mistletoe.

"Hmm." Her aunt was clearly not convinced. "Shall I see them with you? I would like to meet the great Mr. Darcy of Pemberley."

"Would you please? I was not expecting them to come here."

"Of course. Can you tell me anything about Miss Darcy, something that might help me make conversation?"

Elizabeth hesitated. "She seems shy. I understand she is a gifted pianist, but is hesitant to play for others. And it is best not to ask how we came to meet, though I will tell you later if you wish."

Her aunt's eyebrows rose. "I see. I will ask for a tea tray - with our best tea! Let me see to that, and I will meet you here again."

After Elizabeth made the introductions, Georgiana appeared tongue-tied, but Mr. Darcy asked all the proper questions about whether her family was in good health.

Elizabeth said, "It is a pleasure to see you again so soon. I had thought you were still away." There, that avoided saying where they had been.

"We had intended it so, but circumstances changed our plans," Darcy said.

Circumstances. Had he been afraid of discovery? "Have you heard anything further about Mr. Bingley's plans?"

"He is arriving at Netherfield tomorrow and hoping to call on neighbors soon. In his last note, he expressed interest in seeing how Twelfth Night is celebrated there."

Elizabeth smiled. "I believe he may depend upon an invitation from my mother."

"He would be delighted by that." And then Darcy seemed lost for words, though his eyes remained fixed on her.

Georgiana appeared to gather all her courage to say, "Mrs. Gardiner, I understand you spent part of your youth in Derbyshire." She had clearly rehearsed the line.

Mrs. Gardiner beamed at her. "Indeed so! I lived in Lambton, not far from Pemberley, and still have a soft spot for that part of the world. I love all the opportunities of London, but how I miss the hills and dales! Mr. Darcy, I believe you may have been acquainted with my brother in his younger days."

Oh, how Elizabeth hated seeing that cautious look come across Darcy's face! But he seemed to overcome it, for he asked, "What is your brother's name?"

"John Carlisle. Our father was the rector at Lambton. He used to fill in for services at Pemberley when old Mr. Hartfield was ill."

A flash of surprise lit his eyes. "John Carlisle? He shared lessons with me for nearly a year."

"Yes, your father offered that as a great favor when mine was trying to determine whether it was worth the expense of sending John off to school. He was always the best at his studies in the village school, but that was not enough of a recommendation."

"Well, it was obvious to me that he was more than ready! A brilliant fellow, your brother. My tutor was happy to have him since his achievements pushed me to work harder. What is he doing now?"

"He is a barrister here in town. Our father had hoped he would follow him into the ministry, but John wanted more of a challenge. He is still frighteningly clever."

"Pray give him my regards. I recall your father, too. I found his sermons more stimulating than what I was accustomed to."

Was this truly Mr. Darcy, praising commoners? And admitting that Mrs. Gardiner's brother was a better student than he?

The conversation, guided by Mrs. Gardiner, flowed easily for a few minutes. Then she said, "Miss Darcy, our acquaintance is very slight, but I wonder if I might impose upon you to assist me in a small matter. My daughter, who is just ten years of age, is distraught over her pianoforte lesson. Her master is away for the winter, and there is one segment of her lesson that she simply cannot seem to master. She is begging to give up the lessons completely, which would be a shame as she is rather good for her age and has enjoyed it until now."

"Oh, the poor girl! I know how she feels." Miss Darcy hesitated. "I do not know if I can do anything to help, but I would be happy to speak to her and encourage her if you wish."

"I would be so grateful! She does not listen to me on the subject, as I am not a musician myself, but a fashionable young lady like you would be a different matter." She rose to her feet. "Would you be so kind as to join me?"

A brief, uncomfortable silence fell as her aunt left the room with Georgiana. Elizabeth swallowed, her mouth dry. How could she think of anything but that extraordinary kiss? She wanted to call her aunt back, simply to relieve the tension. Darcy seemed content simply to watch her in silence, so it was going to be up to her.

She gathered her courage and said, "Your sister told me you intended to stay in Hertfordshire until Twelfth Night." Oh, dear, had that sounded like an accusation?

"We had intended it so, but Bingley's return changed our plans. Once he was in residence at Netherfield, we could not remain in seclusion there. We could have moved to the main house and pretended to be new arrivals, but my sister did not feel ready to join in convivial society." The corners of his mouth tilted up slightly. "That you were a draw I cannot deny. Georgiana found our stay less appealing without your presence there." His eyes were dark and intent on her, as if there was a secret message for her in his words.

Her cheeks grew warm, but she sternly reminded her body that Mr. Darcy considered her far beneath him and thought her not handsome enough to dance with. He had nothing at stake if he decided to flirt with her, but she would be asking for disappointment if she took him seriously. So she seized on the neutral subject her aunt had raised and began to speak about her young cousin and her pianoforte lessons, which led naturally into the general subject of music.

Where was Mrs. Gardiner? Surely she knew Elizabeth would be embarrassed to be alone with Mr. Darcy for so long!

The sound of the pianoforte tinkling provided a relief. It started with the uneven notes of an early student, and then switched to what was clearly Georgiana's more skilled hands, making pleasant listening even if the music was simple. Thankfully, Elizabeth could allow the conversation to lapse while she played.

Mrs. Gardiner returned while the music continued. "Well!" she said briskly. "I am most grateful to your sister, Mr. Darcy. She not only helped Margaret work through the fingering that was giving her such trouble, but she performed the piece for her, and now they are happily playing duets. I thought of suggesting that you might be waiting for her, but they were having such a fine time that I could not bring myself to interrupt."

"I am the one who should be thanking you," Darcy said gravely. "It is good to hear my sister playing for pleasure again. Of late it has been more of a duty to her."

How remarkable, that he should be admitting so much to a woman he had only just met! Had his old acquaintance with her brother and father had made Mrs. Gardiner more tolerable to him?

"Then we have all helped each other," said Mrs. Gardiner. "Just as it should be. I hope you did not mind my asking her for assistance, Mr. Darcy. It is not something I would normally do with a caller, but I thought your sister might be more comfortable in a less formal setting."

"Apparently you were correct," Darcy said. "I am hoping you could help us in another way, too. Might you be willing to spare your niece for an afternoon? My sister wishes to visit some shops, and would be glad of her friend's company. They would not be on their own; I would accompany them as far as the shops, but I am not considered qualified to give opinions on ribbons and bonnets."

Elizabeth felt heat rise in her cheeks. Even though he was only asking for his sister's sake, that he would be willing to seek her out in *Cheapside*, of all places! And this from the gentleman who had pronounced her no more than tolerable? The question was whether his opinion had truly changed, or if it just showed how desperate he was to help Georgiana.

"Lizzy?" her aunt asked. "It is up to you, of course. If you wish to have an outing with Miss Darcy, I have no objection."

Indifferent. She needed to sound as if this did not matter to her. "I would be glad of a chance to see the shops."

Darcy looked relieved. "Would tomorrow suit you? Or would another day be better? My sister is eager to go out before Twelfth Night."

"I have no fixed plans, so tomorrow would work."

The performance seemed to have come to an end, and a minute later the two young musicians appeared, hand in hand.

"Did you hear that, Lizzy? Mama? Did it not sound marvelous?" Margaret said.

"Indeed it did," Elizabeth agreed. "You played well together."

"Miss Darcy can play *anything*!" Margaret declared.

Georgiana gave a half-smile. "Some things, at least. Your duets were ones I studied years ago. I have some other ones at home, if you would like to try them."

Margaret's eyes lit up. "Oh, yes! Could we play together again someday?"

Her mother intervened. "Miss Darcy no doubt has a great many demands upon her time."

Georgiana shook her head. "I would like that. We enjoyed ourselves, did we not, Miss Gardiner?"

"So much!"

For the first time in his life, Darcy wished that there were no limit on the proper duration of a call. He would have liked to stay longer, breathing in the pleasure of being in Elizabeth's presence and watching her vibrant expressions.

Young Miss Gardiner seemed to share his opinion, though for a different reason. "I wish you did not have to leave! May I walk you to your carriage?" She had already grabbed Georgiana's hand, just in case her new hero refused.

Darcy let them go ahead, following more slowly with Elizabeth by his side, her fragrance of lavender drifting over him. He said softly, "Your family seems to have a gift for setting my sister at ease. I am grateful for it."

"Not what you expected to find in this part of town?" she teased, but with a slight edge to her voice.

"Not something I expected to find anywhere. Generosity of spirit seems to be in short supply these days."

"It is the season of goodwill, after all," she said lightly. "You may have been looking in the wrong places."

That was certainly true. Any goodwill that was present among the *ton* always had a price associated with it. But they had reached the door, so all he could do was thank her for receiving them. As he stepped out the door, he had to force himself not to look back at her.

Amazingly, Georgiana was still smiling as Darcy took his seat across from her in the carriage. "That was good of you to help Mrs. Gardiner's daughter," he said.

"Oh, it was my pleasure. Such a sweet girl! Our duets may have been simple, but it was the first time I enjoyed playing in so long. Even though I was making mistakes, since I hardly remembered the pieces. She seemed to love it anyway."

"We all notice our own mistakes far more than anyone else's." How much had it meant to her to have someone look up to her so admiringly, someone who wanted nothing more than to spend more time with her? Perhaps he should not try so hard to encourage her to interact with the ladies of the *ton*.

Her brow furrowed. "It is not just that. I felt as if no one there would care if I made mistakes, that they would like me just as well. That they would never think to make fun of me as soon as my back is turned." She sighed. "Playing with Margaret was almost like having a sister." Then she looked directly at him. "I wish Miss Elizabeth were my sister."

Darcy stiffened. It was clear she was sending him a message, not mentioning an idle fancy. Should he pretend not to understand it, when for once she was telling him how she felt?

No, it was not worth the risk. "I wish that were possible." And oh, how he ached for it, for his own sake! "Despite her many fine qualities, for the sake of our family,

I must marry someone in high society, with much better connections." And a large dowry to make up for the expense of Georgiana's, too, but he did not want to say that.

Her shoulders drooped. "The ladies in the *ton* care only about your wealth and social status. They pretend to like you only for what they can get from you, just like *he* pretended to like me. Is that truly what you wish for?"

Stung, he said, "Do you think Miss Elizabeth is any different? That she would not want the advantages I could offer her?"

"She befriended me when she had absolutely nothing to gain from it. And when she discovered I was your sister, she tried to run away, rather than using me to get closer to you. That is just the opposite of the girls who claim to be my friend in order to get your attention. I *hate* them and their false friendship."

He stared at her in bafflement. What could he say? There were so many considerations in choosing a wife, and Elizabeth met none of the criteria, neither in her birth, her connections, her education, or her style. Everyone would think him a fool if he married her. His family would scorn her.

Except for Georgiana, who saw her as the one true heart in her world.

His sister was right. How were the young ladies of the marriage mart, dressed up in their silks and jewels, paraded for their accomplishments, taught to flatter any rich gentleman who deigned to dance with them, any different from George Wickham, who pursued Georgiana for her money? How often had he heard from older men at the club, bemoaning that they had married a pretty young girl who could fill their homes with her musical performances, only to have her stop practicing as soon as the vows were taken?

Elizabeth had picked a quarrel with him. She had told him how he had hurt her sister by warning Bingley off her. She had not sought out his good opinion - quite the opposite! If anything, it seemed she only tolerated him for Georgiana's sake.

But then there had been that kiss under the mistletoe. Her lovely eyes had been soft and dark afterwards, her cheeks delightfully flushed. She had not been indifferent to his kiss.

The kiss he had relived a thousand times since then, that he could still feel through his entire body whenever he looked at Elizabeth.

He took a deep breath. "I understand your point, but pray recall that not everyone in the *ton* is shallow and venal. There are good people there, too. Cousin Richard, for example. He wants a wealthy wife, but he has no intention of lying to get one, and he will make some heiress a fine husband."

Georgiana turned her face as if to look out the window, her smile disappearing as if it had never existed. "I suppose."

Damnation! Why did this have to be so hard? Elizabeth always seemed to know the right thing to say to her. But he, despite knowing her all these years, did not.

Chapter 7

THE AFTERNOON OF SHOPPING was off to a good start. Elizabeth had dressed with care, suspecting that the shops involved would be a finer quality than she usually patronized. She did not want to embarrass Georgiana by looking like a poor relation.

If there was someone else she hoped would notice her improved appearance, she did not let herself admit it.

As she had expected, the shops were beyond her budget, but it was still a pleasure to see such fine goods. Her eyes were caught by a pair of exquisitely embroidered kid gloves which she longed to have as her own, but dared not even ask the price. When she saw Mr. Darcy watching her, she reluctantly set them aside.

Then they went to a milliner's shop. Elizabeth was following Miss Darcy when the girl stopped short in the entrance and gasped. Elizabeth craned her neck to look past her at an all too familiar man at the counter. A plain but richly dressed young lady of sixteen or so clung to his arm. Wickham was smiling down at her with what Elizabeth could now recognize as a practiced charm.

"Thank you for allowing me buy it for you," he said. "After all, it will give me such pleasure to see you wearing it, for it frames your beauty."

He had said almost the same words to her once about some ribbons, before she had informed him she could not possibly receive a present from a gentleman. Why had she not realized then that he had no honor? Instead, she had been flattered. What a fool she had been!

Oh, she had some words to say to him! But first she had to protect Miss Darcy from him. The poor girl's face was white. She leaned forward and whispered to her, "Shall we go? There are other shops we can patronize."

"No," she said clearly, though her voice trembled a bit. "I like the bonnets here."

Wickham turned, a delighted expression on his face. Elizabeth was still in the shadow of the doorway, so he might not see her. "Miss Darcy! This is the most pleasant surprise. I cannot tell you how often I have thought of you since our last meeting."

Miss Darcy raised her chin. "Mr. Wickham, what a great pity it is that such a handsome face and charm of manner should be wasted on a man with no more honor than a ... a pig in a sty." The words they had prepared together.

His look of shock was quickly replaced by one of sad concern. "My dear Miss Darcy, what has happened? I fear your brother has been maligning me. He chased me away, you know. I would never have left of my own free will. You must know that."

The girl swallowed hard, apparently having exhausted her strength. Elizabeth was glad to take over. "I suppose you did not leave *me* of your own free will, either. No, you left because you were expelled by the militia for dishonorable behavior with the colonel's wife - and for racking up enormous debts with the town merchants." She turned to the milliner. "Good sir, for your sake, I would strongly urge you not to extend credit to this gentleman. Any tradesman in Meryton would second my suggestion with great vigor."

Not that she had needed to add that, since he had already been bundling away the hatbox out of Wickham's reach. But she had enjoyed saying it nonetheless.

Miss Darcy stepped forward and spoke directly to Wickham's companion. "We have not been introduced, but out of female solidarity, I must warn you that this man's blandishments mean nothing. His manners are so charming, yet he cares about nothing except your dowry. Pray take care."

Just then, an older woman hurried into the shop. "There you are, Sophia! Oh, Mr. Wickham," she simpered. "I did not see you there."

The girl named Sophia straightened. "I would like to leave now, Mama. I fear we may have been sadly misled in Mr. Wickham's character." She marched away from him without a backwards glance and out the door.

Wickham's face twisted. "This is all Darcy's fault, damn him!"

A deep voice spoke behind Elizabeth. "I dearly wish I could take credit, but this is purely the work of the ladies. They both deserve medals for their impressive efforts. Sister, Miss Elizabeth, would you like to leave now?"

Georgiana's face took on a look of stubborn determination reminiscent of her brother. "No, I thank you. I came in here to look at bonnets, and I will not let *that person* chase me away."

"Nor I," said Elizabeth loyally, though Mr. Wickham's furious glare burned into her. "Oh, look at that one over there, with the turquoise ribbon! It would bring out your eyes beautifully."

The shopkeeper, with a quick scowl at Mr. Wickham, hurried to help them.

Chapter 8

WHEN ELIZABETH WAS SHOWN into the drawing room at Darcy House, Georgiana was the only one there. She should have felt relieved, after all her dread of running into Mr. Darcy on this visit. Why was disappointment welling up in her instead?

She did her best to hide it, smiling warmly at Georgiana as she greeted her. After all, the girl was the one she had come to see, not her silent, disapproving brother. Even if he had not seemed so disapproving of late.

She had not wanted to call at Darcy House at all. Seeing Mr. Darcy again would not be a good idea. But there was no way to avoid it, not after Georgiana had cried in her arms after their encounter with Mr. Wickham, and then confided the entire story of their encounter. If Elizabeth did not return, the girl would have blamed herself for shocking her new friend.

Besides, she had a message to deliver. One that would be easier when Georgiana's brother was not present.

After they had chatted for a few minutes, Elizabeth said, "My aunt has a question. She understands what it is to be going through a difficult time and wanting to avoid society, and she does not wish to put any pressure on you to do something that would make you uncomfortable. But, if you thought you might enjoy it, she would be happy to invite you to the family's Twelfth Night celebration. It is not a formal occasion at all, with no other guests except two of my uncle's young apprentices who have no family here to spend the holiday with. All the children will be part of it, too, as long as they can stay awake, so it will indubitably be a very silly time with them running about." Elizabeth hesitated. "I almost did not mention it because I imagine your brother would think it quite beneath you, but my aunt's instincts are usually good, and she said sometimes we all need an event which includes child's play."

"Does the invitation include my brother as well?" Georgiana asked shyly.

"If you wish it. He might find it trying, though, and unlike his usual company." Surely they had been through enough that she could speak the truth to the girl. "I would not want him to feel obligated to come." The idea of Mr.

Darcy looming disapprovingly over the company would ruin it for her.

"Oh, he will not! I will fetch him, and we can ask." The girl hurried from the room.

Why had she not simply sent a servant for him? Was it not their job?

But she had little time to ponder this mysterious behavior, for within a few minutes, Mr. Darcy appeared in the doorway.

Alone. Without Georgiana.

Elizabeth's pulse quickened. Was the tell-tale color rising in her cheeks? They felt warm.

He bowed and asked after the Gardiners' health. Even though they were in trade! Could it be for her sake?

"My sister tells me you have a question for me," he said.

"It is more in the nature of an invitation, actually. A rather impertinent invitation at that, but you will hardly be surprised by that, since it is coming from me." Elizabeth tilted her head. How would he respond to her teasing?

"I cannot imagine being disappointed in anything you offer, whether impertinent or not," he said mildly.

Well, best to just spit it out, rather than leave him guessing something far worse than it was. "My aunt and uncle are having a family Twelfth Night celebration, and Mrs. Gardiner has invited you and your sister to join us. I believe she was thinking more of Miss Darcy, though you were included in the invitation. She hoped it might lift her spirits. We will certainly understand if you do not wish to join her, given the nature of the event. There will be no fashionable people and a great many very silly games."

"We would both be delighted to attend, and I pray you to give my thanks to Mrs. Gardiner," he said. And it sounded as if he meant it.

Now Elizabeth's cheeks were definitely hot. "I must warn you that you are unlikely to find it interesting, sir. This is more of a children's party than anything else. One to which you would be unwise to wear your best clothes, as spills will indubitably happen and you might have a grubby child clinging to your leg." Truly, it would be better if he did not come. Even if something about the idea of Mr. Darcy holding a child made her heart thump.

"I believe my valet will be up to the task of handling whatever happens," he said dryly.

She tried again. "Even the adults will be playing games, taking on foolish roles."

"I am familiar with Twelfth Night revels, Miss Elizabeth. I have even been known to enjoy them."

She stared at him in perplexity. She had expected him to be glad to have an easy escape from this invitation. "The reason I invited your sister, over certain qualms of my own, was because of something my aunt said. She told me it would be good for a girl who had been forced to grow up too fast to have a chance to be a child again, even if only for an evening."

He nodded slowly. "There may be something to that. It seemed like no time between when Georgiana was playing with dolls and when she was ready to elope."

Elope? Had it gone so far? Poor girl! "I agree. But I am aware you found the company at the Meryton assembly less than pleasant, so I wonder what you will make of having to share a table with apprentices and overtired, unruly children. My cousins are usually well behaved, but the holiday excitement may be too much for them."

He took a step towards her and placed his forefinger lightly beneath her chin, and suddenly she fell back in time to that moment under the mistletoe. Her lips tingled with the memory, and her insides grew hot.

But instead of kissing her, he asked softly, "You seem eager to dissuade me. Do you wish me to stay away, Miss Elizabeth?"

Her body had turned traitor, and she could not think. So she blurted out, "No, but I fear you will disapprove of us, and I would not like that."

A slight smile quirked his lips. "You need not worry about that. I may not be as accustomed to children as you, but I assure you I will be happy with the company." Something about how he said it, the soft look in his dark eyes, told her he was not speaking about the children.

The air around them suddenly seemed thick, and she had to work to suck in a breath of air. "Then we will be glad to have you, although you may regret it when you see my uncle on his hands and knees playing horsey with the little ones."

Now his smile grew wider. "That might be beyond my skills, but my cousin's children have found my pick-a-back rides to be tolerable."

She could not help teasing. "Then you may be in great demand after all, Mr. Darcy."

He said, in barely more than a whisper, "I can only hope."

Chapter 9

ELIZABETH HAD GIVEN UP trying to convince herself that she did not care about having Darcy's good opinion. How could she do otherwise, when she had spent the night dreaming of Darcy tipping up her chin with his finger – and not stopping there? Her lips tingled every time she thought about it.

That did not stop her from laughing each time her aunt suggested Darcy might have a *tendre* for her, as if such a notion were completely ridiculous. She had her pride, after all. Nothing could come of this, and she did not want anyone pitying her for disappointed hopes.

Still, the anticipation of the evening haunted her all day on Twelfth Night, so she was glad when their guests finally arrived. Her eyes immediately flew to Darcy. He had taken her advice and was dressed plainly, if still elegantly, and her mouth went dry at the sight of him. She tore her gaze away to greet Georgiana with enthusiasm, though her efforts were drowned out by little Margaret's delight at Miss Darcy's appearance.

Georgiana offered a thin paper-wrapped packet to the girl. "I brought you a Twelfth Night gift. It may be for both of us someday."

Margaret's eyes went wide. "For me?" She tore open the paper with more enthusiasm than regard for manners, revealing a booklet of sheet music. "Duets? Will you play them with me, once I have learnt them?" she asked earnestly.

"That is my intention," Georgiana said. "These are ones I played when I was your age. Miss Elizabeth, this is for you."

It was a smaller package. "How very kind of you!" Elizabeth exclaimed, grateful that Mrs. Gardiner had warned her this might be a possibility.

"I hope you will like it." Now Georgiana sounded shy.

"I am certain I will," Elizabeth said warmly as she unwrapped it, and then she gasped. Inside lay the kid gloves she had admired at the shop, the ones far too expensive for her. A generous gift indeed, and her cheeks warmed because she knew precisely who had picked it out. Mr. Darcy had been watching her when she picked up those very gloves and stroked them longingly. "These are beautiful! I thank you. I love the embroidery – I have always wanted a design like this. I will treasure them." She did not dare look at Darcy.

"I am so glad you like them." Georgiana said. "They are from both of us."

Elizabeth caught her breath. Even though gloves were one of the few things a single gentleman could properly give to a lady he was not engaged to, it felt more intimate than that. She would never be able to slip these on her hands without thinking of him. "Then I thank you both! And I have a small thing for you, Miss Darcy, though it can hardly compare." She had spent all morning finishing the embroidery on a bookmark just in case this happened.

Before she could even fetch it, Margaret grabbed Georgiana's hand. "Come into the party," she cried. "It is almost time to draw lots for our characters!"

Mr. Darcy said solemnly, "We certainly cannot miss that."

Elizabeth let out a breath. He might do well here after all.

The Gardiners' Twelfth Night gathering was more enjoyable than Darcy had expected. Being in Elizabeth's presence was, as always, both a delight and a torment. John Carlisle, Mrs. Gardiner's brother and Darcy's childhood lesson-mate, had stopped by at the beginning solely to meet him again. He proved as stimulating a conversation-alist as he had ever been, and a reminder of the happy days when both Darcy's parents had still been alive. He suggested another meeting to catch up with Darcy in a quieter place, and Darcy had been glad to agree.

The children and the apprentices were indeed noisy as they played their Twelfth Night characters. Darcy suspect-ed Mrs. Gardiner's hand in it when he had chosen the lot making him king for the evening, if only to avoid any of the youngsters having the role. Little Margaret started out as his queen, but she had abandoned him quickly in favor of Georgiana, her clear favorite.

Not that he had minded; it meant he could sit next to Elizabeth. Since he was king for the night, no one could gainsay him when he chose that seat. But now Margaret had called Elizabeth over to her, and as queen, she could not be refused. Darcy's eyes followed her as she wove her way across the crowded room to her little cousin.

How was he ever to forget her? It had been hard enough when she was a mere acquaintance, and he could pretend that closer contact would disillusion him. Now, in just a matter of days, she had somehow slipped into his life as the only person Georgiana had confided in, the only person outside his cousin Richard who knew the truth of what had happened in Ramsgate.

Not only was she aware of it, but he suspected she knew more about it even than he did. After their shopping ex-cursion, Elizabeth and Georgiana had disappeared to her rooms for hours. When they had emerged, his sister's face was tear-stained, but she seemed relieved, as if a giant burden had gone from her shoulders.

How could he possibly let Elizabeth go now? His duty demanded it, but it would be like tearing out a bit of his heart.

When she returned to his side, she was wearing Margaret's paper crown, a little worse for wear and slightly askew, along with a wicked smile. "Margaret has abdicated in my favor," she said. "Being queen was leaving her out of all the fun of playing exaggerated characters. Too boring, she says, but apparently she believes I do not mind being bored."

"I find you anything but dull." Why had those words popped out of his mouth? He wished he could blame Mrs. Gardiner's surprisingly strong Twelfth Night punch, but he was far more intoxicated by Elizabeth's presence than any spirited beverage.

"Why, Mr. Darcy! Or should I say Your Majesty?" Her eyes danced. "If I did not know better, I might almost consider that a compliment."

He should not say anything. If he paid her more compliments, she might think he was courting her. And, God help him, he was no longer completely certain he was not.

How had that happened?

Something in his expression must have troubled her, for her smile faded away. "Pray excuse me, sir. My aunt is beckoning me, and I suspect she wishes my help with little Edward."

She did not wait for an answer, simply walking away towards Mrs. Gardiner, who was holding an exhausted toddler to her shoulder. They conversed briefly, and then Elizabeth took the child from her and headed out into the vestibule.

Without even a second glance at him.

Why, oh why, had he suddenly been tongue-tied at exactly the wrong moment? If only he could follow her and say something, anything, so it did not look like she had embarrassed him. He could not bear having her think that.

Even if he had to say too much. Duty be damned!

It would be beyond improper to go after her, so he did the next best thing and approached the other young Gardiner boy. Charlie, that was his name. "Would you like another pick-a-back ride?" he asked.

"Oh, yes, please!" the boy piped. "Will you trot and neigh, too?"

"I believe I can." If it would get him out into the vestibule where he could wait for Elizabeth, he would get down on all fours and bark. He bent down so Charlie could climb on his back.

The boy cried, "Hup, horsey!"

And Darcy started to trot, tossing his head like a highly strung mount, making Charlie shriek with delight. As they circled the room, Georgiana watched him with wide but happy eyes. Did she think he had forgotten how to play? He had grown too serious, these last few years.

He made a few rounds, to the boy's glee, and then trotted out into the vestibule. Still mostly in sight of the rest of the party, but where he would be the first to see Elizabeth descending the stairs. He entertained the boy with a series of neighs and snorts, pretending to buck him off.

Finally she appeared, her eyebrows delicately raised at the sight of his lively play. But a small smile danced on her lips, and that made everything worth it.

Darcy gave the boy one last circle of trotting, then lowered him to the ground. "Well ridden," he said, "but your steed is tiring, and your family awaits."

The boy's eyes were shining. "Thank you, sir!" Then he ran off into the parlor.

Darcy seized his moment. "Miss Elizabeth, I pray you will forgive me for being tongue-tied earlier. I fear I gave you the wrong impression."

Her smile widened. "Tongue-tied?" she asked lightly. "I have never seen someone look so shocked to discover they had complimented someone."

"I found myself at a loss for words, Miss Elizabeth, something that never seems to happen to you."

"So now I talk too much?" she teased.

He had to do better this time. "Your eloquence and wit constantly amaze me." He lowered his voice, leaning his head towards her. "And that, Miss Elizabeth, was most definitely a compliment."

Her breath caught. Then her eyes quickly darted upwards, and her cheeks flushed. But she said nothing.

He followed her gaze to the sprig of mistletoe hanging from the ceiling, and his heart beat faster. "We do seem to have a talent for this, do we not?"

She tilted her head. "Or you may have planned it this way."

He shook his head. "I wish I had thought of it, but I have been too well entertained to trouble myself to look upwards. But I find myself quite satisfied with the situation."

"You are taking a great risk, sir," Elizabeth said with mock gravity. "Likely you think that is innocent local mistletoe, but it is from the clump at home – the magical Netherfield mistletoe I gave to my aunt before we left Longbourn. You were fortunate to have escaped its effects once, but they say that a second kiss beneath it is impossible to forget and will haunt you the rest of your days."

As if the first kiss was not still haunting him! Not to mention leaving him longing desperately for another, like a man wandering the desert dreaming of water. But he could not tell her that, so instead he said, "I thought you considered that an old wives' tale."

She teased, "The old wives may have wisdom of their own, and I would not want to see you entrapped against your will." There was a note of sincerity under her teasing.

It was true. She did not want to trap him into marriage. Even if the flush in her cheeks and her darkening eyes suggested that her body wanted something else entirely.

Georgiana had been right. Elizabeth Bennet was a rare gem - one who did not want him for the advantages he could give her. He stepped a little closer until her lavender scent overtook his senses. "What if it is not be against my will?"

Her eyes widened. "I find that difficult to believe."

How could she still be so unsure of his feelings? He could show her, if he could not tell her. "Believe it," he whispered as he lowered his mouth to hers.

This time she tipped her head back to meet him, her lips seeking his. Her eagerness sent a surge of need through him, which only intensified as he tasted her intoxicating sweetness. He luxuriated in her softness, the warmth of her. God, but she was irresistible!

Then her lips opened beneath his. Just a tiny bit, as if she had needed a breath, but his desire surged. She could not know what she was doing. He should not take advantage of it. He should not.

But somehow his tongue was caressing her, urging her to open further. For a moment she hesitated. Had he gone too far? But then she allowed him in, and he lost himself in the heat of her.

The sound of a man clearing his throat woke Darcy from his befuddlement of desire. Elizabeth's hands were pressed against his chest, and they were standing far too close for a public kiss under a mistletoe. Good Lord, his hand was on her hip! What was wrong with him?

Elizabeth Bennet had bewitched him. And all he wanted was to go back to kissing her, to pretend they were not just beyond the open door of a room full of people, including young children.

Somehow, from some reserve, he found the strength to step back from her.

Her uncle, despite being shorter than Darcy, seemed to loom next to him, and his previously genial expression was unsmiling. "Excuse me for interrupting," Mr. Gardiner said coolly, "but I must speak to my niece."

Elizabeth stiffened, the flush fading from her cheeks.

Instinct took over. Darcy took her hand in his. "Pray forgive my inappropriate overenthusiasm," he said. "When Miss Elizabeth and I found ourselves under the mistletoe, she asked me first if my intentions were honorable. I told her they were, if she wished it. It is not every day that a man gets everything he has ever dreamed of, and I fear it went to my head."

Mr. Gardiner studied him searchingly, and then a broad smile crossed his face. "Is that so? I suppose I cannot blame you for that. I have always said it would take an extraordinary man to win Lizzy's heart, and it seems I was correct."

"I would call myself extraordinarily lucky," he said. And he was.

Elizabeth bit her lip. She whispered, "You need not do this."

A joyous recklessness filled him. He glanced pointedly up. "Indeed I do. Netherfield mistletoe, after all. The old wives knew what they were talking about."

Georgiana hurried over then, her hands clasped in front of her, excitement filling her eyes. "Brother, has something happened?"

That was when he realized everyone in the room had fallen silent and was watching them.

Before he could answer, Elizabeth said with a laugh, "You no doubt saw what happened, but before anything further is said, I believe there is a certain question that needs to be asked - and answered. Perhaps in more privacy than we have at the moment."

Mr. Gardiner smiled. "My study is at your disposal." He rubbed his hands together happily. "As it ought to be, since you are the king and queen of the revels."

Could this possibly be real, and not one of those passionate dreams that haunted his nights? Darcy followed Elizabeth as she ushered him into a cozy room lined with bookshelves. A dark wood desk dominated it. But Darcy could only think of Elizabeth.

As she closed the door behind her, there was a certain sadness in her eyes. Before he could speak, she said, "First I must ask you one question. Are you doing this for your sister's sake?"

Why was she questioning him rather than happily accepting the best offer she would ever receive? Because Elizabeth Bennet would never follow those rules, and he loved her for it. "No," he said huskily. "If you are asking whether Georgiana would like to have you as her sister, the answer is yes. Has she said as much to me? Also yes. Would I consider marrying a woman for her sake? No."

She bit her lip. "I have seen what happens when a marriage is undertaken between two people because of a temporary advantage, rather than out of a similarity of spirit. Your sister will marry someday and leave you, and you would be stuck with me for the rest of your life. Do you truly want that?"

"More than anything." And it was true, so true. He longed to take her home with him that very night and never leave her side. "Do you not know that I have been fascinated with you almost since the beginning? I could barely take my eyes off you. I was glad to leave Netherfield with Bingley because I knew I could not resist you much longer, but you came to me in my dreams. I could not forget you, even for an hour. When I walked into that cottage at Netherfield, wondering who was performing the miracle of making my sister laugh, there you were. I knew then that I could never forget you."

Her flush deepened. "Well, then." Was the astonishingly articulate Elizabeth Bennet actually lost for words? "I had no idea. I knew only that you had not found me handsome enough to dance with at the assembly."

How could he ever have thought such a thing? "I was in poor spirits that evening. Once I spoke with you, once you had crossed wits with me, I saw something very different."

She laughed shakily. "I suppose, then... that does put a different light on it."

"Will you, then, do me the great honor of becoming my wife?" He tried to put all his feeling into his voice. He, who had always thought any woman would be thrilled to receive his proposal, now knew differently. "Do you think you could learn to care for me, at least a little?"

She cast her eyes down, and his heart began to pound at the fear she might refuse him. But instead she said slowly, "A month ago I would have said it was impossible, when I thought you looked at me only to criticize and blamed you for separating Mr. Bingley from my sister. But over these twelve days of Christmas - and a few before - I have seen another gentleman than the one I thought I knew." She took a deep breath. "My feelings now are different, and I will be proud to accept your offer with the hope of a future of knowing you even better."

There was nothing to be done for it. Without even thinking of what he was doing, he swept her into his arms again, drinking deep of her lips.

A child's voice interrupted them. "Oh, ick, Lizzy!"

Darcy jumped back. It was Charlie, the little boy he had carried earlier on his back, who apparently had a terrible sense of timing.

Now the child pushed between them and took Elizabeth by her hand. "Papa says it is time for you to return."

Elizabeth gave a shaky laugh. "Let me guess. We were being too quiet."

"Yes, that is what he said," the boy agreed, with a complete lack of embarrassment. "Besides, it is time for the pudding, and you would not want to miss that."

Elizabeth widened her eyes dramatically. "The pudding? Of course not. How could anything be as delicious as the pudding?" And then she gave Darcy a mischievous look that told him exactly what she thought was more delicious than any Twelfth Night dessert.

Epilogue

F INALLY THE MOMENT HAD arrived, the one Darcy
had been longing for, when they left the church and
he could help Elizabeth into his carriage – *their* carriage! –
and drive away with her as man and wife. No day in his life
could ever be finer than this one.

But before he could even hold out his hand to his bride,
Georgiana came running up to them and threw her arms
around Elizabeth. "I am so happy you are my sister in truth
now! This is the most perfect gift I have ever received."

"I am glad, too. But none of us can be as pleased as my
cousin Margaret, who simply cannot believe her good for-
tune that you are now part of her family," Elizabeth teased.
"Just think of all the trouble you can get into together!"

To Darcy's delight, Georgiana laughed. His sister had turned a corner that day she had confronted Wickham in the shop. Her spirits were higher, and she was playing the piano at home again. Most astonishingly, she had agreed to come with him to Netherfield when he followed Elizabeth here, even though it meant being among society again. She had retreated to her room more than once when it became too much for her, but more often she had been in company. And she loved going to Longbourn to visit Elizabeth, even among her great crowd of boisterous sisters.

For his sister's sake, Darcy was glad he had not given into his first impulse to insist on marrying Elizabeth immediately after that wondrous Twelfth Night when Elizabeth had consented to be his. He would have happily gone out the next morning to buy a license. To his dismay, the Gardiners had advised against it. Strongly.

Even more dismaying, he suspected they were right.

Mr. Gardiner had said, "I understand why you kept your second visit to Netherfield a secret. But I beg you to consider how this will look to Mr. Bennet when you ask his permission. As far as he knows, you left Netherfield with Mr. Bingley with no intention to return and Lizzy expressing no fondness for you. Then you suddenly appear six weeks later to ask for his daughter's hand. He could draw some unfortunate conclusions from that."

It would be completely unacceptable. "What would you suggest, then?"

"Lizzy could write home tomorrow with the news that she encountered you and your sister here in London and invited you both here for Twelfth Night. Next week, she can tell them about further encounters. My wife can mention being favorably impressed with you. When Lizzy returns to Longbourn in a fortnight, you can follow, paying her marked attention. Then a proposal will not seem so shocking."

Mrs. Gardiner had added, "I must put in a word for Lizzy, too. Your affection for her, Mr. Darcy, appears to be of some standing, but from what I can tell, she only changed her mind about you a fortnight ago. I would urge you to give her time to know you better before you announce the engagement."

Elizabeth said, "I assure you, Aunt, I am quite certain."

"Then it will not harm you to wait a few weeks," her uncle had replied. "Marriage is not to be entered into lightly."

That quote from the wedding service itself could not be argued with.

Still, every day of these six weeks had seemed to last forever, except for the happy moments when he was in Elizabeth's company. Those had fled past. But he was still glad they had waited,

because the Netherfield mistletoe had won yet another feather in its cap. Soon after Bingley had stolen a kiss from Jane Bennet under the sprig at Longbourn, she had made him the second happiest man in the world.

Darcy, of course, claimed the position of happiest.

Sharing the wedding ceremony with his friend and her sister made it an altogether delightful event. Mr. and Mrs. Bingley were still on the church steps, but they had only a few miles to travel to Netherfield. Darcy and Elizabeth would be going to London, where they would spend a month or two of newlywed joy before traveling to Pemberley when the weather improved.

As if on cue, a few lazy snowflakes drifted down, catching on Elizabeth's bonnet. She put out her free hand to catch one on her embroidered glove, the very one he had given on her on that fateful Twelfth Night. She looked up at him with an impish smile that would brighten the cloudiest day.

"I believe that is a hint that we should be on the road before it gets any worse, my love," he said, and helped her up the folding steps into the carriage. He had given orders for warm bricks for their feet and lap blankets, and he suspected they would be grateful for both.

Or his new bride could keep him warm.

As he stepped up behind her, she said, "If I had seen you smile so widely when we first met, I would have had quite a different impression of you!"

He sat down beside her and arranged the heavy blankets over their legs. "It would not have taken the magical Netherfield mistletoe to make you give me a second look, then?" he teased.

"Or the old-wives-tale mistletoe," she said with mock austerity.

He laughed. "In either case, I am not complaining. I will be forever grateful for it." He rapped his cane head on the roof of the carriage.

As it swayed into motion, Elizabeth laid her forefinger against her lips. "The question is..."

"What is it?"

Her lovely eyes danced. "The question is whether it will be just as magical to kiss you when there is no Netherfield mistletoe overhead."

He placed his arm around her shoulders and pulled her close, glad of the wedding ring that finally allowed him to do so. "Well, my love, for the sake of knowledge, perhaps we should find out."

Also by Abigail Reynolds

Spellbound at Pemberley

The Magic of Pemberley

The Guardians of Pemberley

The Price of Pride

A Matter of Honor

Mr. Darcy's Enchantment

Conceit & Concealment

Mr. Darcy's Journey

Alone with Mr. Darcy

The Darcys of Derbyshire

Mr. Darcy's Noble Connections
To Conquer Mr. Darcy
What Would Mr. Darcy Do?
By Force of Instinct
Mr. Darcy's Undoing
Mr. Fitzwilliam Darcy: The Last Man in the World
The Man Who Loved Pride & Prejudice
Morning Light
Mr. Darcy's Obsession
A Pemberley Medley
Mr. Darcy's Letter
The Darcy Brothers (co-author)
Mr. Darcy and the Enchanted Library (co-author)

About the author

ABIGAIL REYNOLDS MAY BE a nationally bestselling author and a physician, but she can't follow a straight line with a ruler. Originally from upstate New York, she studied Russian and theater at Bryn Mawr College and marine biology at the Marine Biological Laboratory in Woods Hole. After a stint in performing arts administration, she decided to attend medical school, and took up writing as a hobby during her years as a physician in private practice.

A life-long lover of Jane Austen's novels, Abigail began writing variations on *Pride & Prejudice* in 2001, then expanded her repertoire to include a series of novels set on her beloved Cape Cod. Her books have won multiple awards and several have been national bestsellers. Her most recent releases are *Spellbound at Pemberley*, *The Magic of Pemberley*, *The Price of Pride*, and *Mr. Darcy's Enchantment*. You can find her other books listed on her Author Page at Amazon. Her books have been translated into seven languages. She lives on Cape Cod with her family and a menagerie of animals. Her hobbies do not include sleeping or cleaning her house.

Visit Abigail's website at Pemberley Variations

Acknowledgments

T HIS NOVELLA OWES ITS existence to Cristina
Huelsz of Cris Translates, who asked me to write
a Austenesque Christmas short story for an antholo-
gy to benefit Jane Austen's House on Jane Austen's
250th birthday. Since I support the cause, I said I'd try,
but couldn't promise anything since I've never written
a Christmas story and short stories are a challenge for
my Muse, which likes complicated tales. I was half-way
through the story when I realized it was already three times
Cristy's maximum length. I carved off the first few scenes
and put a simple ending on it, and then sent it off. Somehow, though, the rest of the story wanted to be told, and

this novella is the result. The much shorter version of it can be found in Christmas Celebrations 2025.

Many thanks to my betas, Debbie Fortin, Nicola Geiger, and Lori Orcena, for catching typos and missing words. My critique partners in Bluestockings without Borders helped with many of the details, including Sarah Shepherd suggested the title. All remaining errors are mine.

www.ingramcontent.com/pod-product-compliance
Lightning Source LLC
Chambersburg PA
CBHW052016170626
46808CB00007B/2954